The Rabbit's Tale

Retold by Lynne Benton

Illustrated by Fred Blunt

Reading consultant: Alison Kelly
University of Roehampton

Rabbit was sad.

His home was too small.

"I need more room,"
he said.

"Owl is clever. Maybe
he can help."

He went to see Owl.

Owl thought.

"Ask your brothers and sisters to stay," he said.

Rabbit was puzzled,

but he did as Owl said.

All his brothers and sisters came.

12

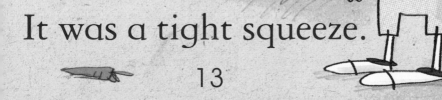

It was a tight squeeze.

Rabbit went
back to Owl.

Owl smiled. "Ask all your friends too."

"Really?" said Rabbit.
But he did.

All his friends came.

He ran to Owl.

21

Everyone went home.

Rabbit was happy.

PUZZLES

Puzzle 1

Can you spot the differences
between these two pictures?

There are six to find.

Puzzle 2

Look at the pictures and put them in order:

A

B

C

D

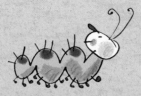

Puzzle 3

What are Rabbit and Owl doing? Choose the right word for the picture:

reading   thinking

sweeping   jumping

A  B

C  D

Answers to puzzles

Puzzle 1

Puzzle 2 - C A D B

C

A

D

B

Puzzle 3

A - sweeping

B - thinking

C - jumping

D - reading

About the story

The Rabbit's Tale is based on a European folk tale. There are lots of different versions of the story. Sometimes it is an old man or woman whose home is too small.

Designed by Caroline Spatz
Series editor: Lesley Sims
Series designer: Russell Punter

First published in 2012 by Usborne Publishing Ltd., Usborne House,
83-85 Saffron Hill, London EC1N 8RT, England. www.usborne.com
Copyright © 2012 Usborne Publishing Ltd.